This book belongs to

_____

For the real Ali, who challenges me every day to look at the world differently.

Copyright 2021 Laura Hatchell

ISBN: 978-1-9163651-3-1 (paperback)
ISBN: 978-1-9163651-4-8 (hardcover)

First Edition Book, September 2021

Book cover design, illustration, editing, and interior layout by:

www.1000storybooks.com

ALI AND THE FAIRY DOOR

LAURA HATCHELL

Ali's ball sailed through the air and into the trees.

"Back in a minute," she called to her mammy and daddy, then raced after it.

Ali spotted her ball at the foot of an oak tree. Leaves crunched under her feet as she ran to get it – but she stopped in her tracks.

The enormous tree had a strange-looking door carved into its trunk. Curious, she reached out to touch it.

Her hand DISAPPEARED!

Amazed, Ali stepped forward ...

... and found herself on the other side of the door. In a completely different land!

The grass was candyfloss pink, and the sky was filled with the fluffiest clouds. She looked around, confused.

Where was she?

In the distance, she could hear shouting and laughter, and something else too...

She could hear crying.

Ali followed the path, and at the end of the hill she came upon a little girl crying.

"Are you okay?" Ali asked.

The little girl rubbed her eyes. "I hurt my wing, and now I can't play chasing with the other fairies.

"I've never met a real fairy before." Ali sat down and offered her hand. "I'm Ali."

"I'm Ziggy," the fairy said, shaking her hand with a sniffle.

"Can your wing be fixed?"

Ziggy looked glum. "There's a magical blue flower that can heal it, but it only grows in the Dark Forest, and there are all kinds of scary monsters in there."

Ali jumped up. "I'll go with you to the Dark Forest. We'll get the flower together."

"Really?" Ziggy looked at her hopefully.

Ali nodded and Ziggy leapt to her feet, letting out a loud whistle. Two huge bunnies appeared, their ears perked and noses twitching. Ziggy climbed up on one, and Ali climbed aboard the other with a big grin.

It didn't take long to reach the edge of the Dark Forest. Ali shivered as she looked at the shadows dancing between the trees.

She pushed away her nerves and gave Ziggy a confident smile. "Come on."

Leaves rustled and branches creaked as they made their way through the forest.

A shrill shriek made them jump in fright. When a cute little pink ball of fur with three eyes scurried from the bushes, they giggled at their own silliness.

But then, they heard it ...

A loud "ROAR" came from beyond the trees, and a ball of fire shot up in the air.

Ziggy paled and tugged at Ali's arm. "We should go back. I'm scared."

Ali was scared too, but she wanted to help her new friend, so she put her finger to her lips and crept forward to peek through the trees.

Ali gulped. "Is that ..."

Ziggy stared miserably at the field of blue flowers and nodded. "The dragon."

"Maybe I can distract it while you get the flower," Ali suggested, not so confident anymore.

"Oh no." Ziggy shook her head. "I couldn't let you do that. I'd never forgive myself if you were eaten.

As Ali tried to think of a new plan, another noise came from the clearing.

HICCUP!

HICCUP!

HICCUP!

She looked at Ziggy, eyes wide. "The dragon has the hiccups! No wonder he's grumpy." Suddenly excited, Ali added, "I have an idea!"

Before Ziggy could stop her, Ali ran back to the stream they'd passed earlier.

She grabbed the biggest leaf she could find and bent down to scoop up some water.

Very careful not to spill it, Ali made her way back to her friend.

She found Ziggy cowering behind a bush.

"I think we should go," the fairy said, trembling.

Ali just smiled. "It'll be okay."

Ali stepped through the trees and into the clearing.

When the dragon saw her, he let out a loud "ROAR." But he didn't eat her or set her on fire, so that was a good start.

"I won't hurt you. I want to help." Ali edged forward
with the leaf of water.

Ignoring the dragon's glower, she stretched her arms out

The dragon sniffed at her offering suspiciously.
After a moment, he began to lap at the water.

Ali waited patiently until he finished.

A minute passed. No hiccups!

Suddenly, the dragon lumbered forward...

Ali shrieked.

But then she found herself enveloped in a big hug.

Ali giggled with delight and hugged the dragon back.

She told him all about Ziggy's injured wing and the flower they needed.

The dragon plucked the biggest, brightest, bluest flower and handed it to Ali shyly.

When Ali returned with the flower, Ziggy jumped for joy.

Together, they crushed the flower petals and rubbed them onto her injured wing.

Like magic, the wing healed before their eyes.

"I can play chasing with the other fairies now." Ziggy clapped her hands, barely able to contain her excitement. "You have to play too!"

Ali's face fell. "But I don't have any wings."

The dragon let out a soft huff and nudged Ali with his head. He nodded toward his back, and she grinned.

Needless to say, Ali won the game of chasing.

Before long, it was time to say
goodbye to all her new friends.

She promised to visit again soon and stepped back through the fairy door just in time to hear her mammy and daddy call her name.

ABOUT THE AUTHOR

Hailing from the fair isle of potatoes and leprechauns, Laura is mammy to a little girl with a big personality. When she's not working or answering the gazillion questions "why?" from her daughter, she explores imaginary worlds in her mind.

In her spare time, Laura writes urban fantasy for adults, and she is excited to bring the magic and fantasy to a new world she can enjoy with her little girl. Nothing beats the imagination of a child, and we could all stand to be a little more childlike sometimes.